FOOTBALL KIDS

George Sullivan

Illustrated with photographs

COBBLEHILL BOOKS
Dutton   New York

ACKNOWLEDGMENTS

Many people helped in the preparation of this book. Special thanks are due the players profiled for their willingness to participate in the project and for the time they devoted to interviews. Special thanks are also due coach Carlos Gomez, George Washington High School, New York City; Coach Ron Lombardi, Fordham Preparatory School, Bronx, New York; Coach John Mayo, Enrico Fermi High School, Enfield, Connecticut; Bruce Bott, Athletic Director, and Jack Sullivan, Fordham Preparatory School; Bill Travers, New York *Daily News;* Francesca Kurti, TLC Custom Labs, New York City; and Aime LaMontagne.

All photographs are by George Sullivan

Library of Congress Cataloging-in-Publication Data
Sullivan, George, date
    Football kids/George Sullivan; illustrated with photographs.
        p.   cm.
    Summary: Profiles seven high school boys who play football, revealing their likes and dislikes, favorite plays, and individual views of the game.
    ISBN 0–525–65040–7
    1. Football—United States—Juvenile literature.   2. Football players—United States—Juvenile literature—Case studies.   3. School sports—United States—Juvenile literature.   [1. Football players.   2. Football.]   I. Title.
    GV950.7.S89   1990   920—dc20   [796.332'092'2]   [B]   90–33096   CIP   AC

Published in the United States by Cobblehill Books,
an affiliate of Dutton Children's Books, a division
of Penguin Books USA Inc.
Designed by Jean Krulis
Printed in the U.S.A.
First Edition   10 9 8 7 6 5 4 3 2 1

CONTENTS

INTRODUCTION

Football is the best taught subject in American high schools, according to a Brooklyn, New York, teacher. "It is probably the only subject we do not try to make easy," she said.

It's true. In football, the standards are very high. A member of the high school team works much harder on behalf of football than any classroom subject.

Students who want to play football must first learn the rules of the game. Then formations and plays have to be memorized. The physical demands are even greater. From late in August to late in November, players spend long, difficult hours in practice sessions. They roll around on muddy fields and endure the deep chill of gray afternoons. In the final weeks of the season, there may be snow and freezing temperatures. They risk broken limbs and other injuries. They are seldom without pain.

They also have to follow a demanding code of discipline, turning their backs on tobacco, alcohol, and drugs. They have to put strict limits on their social lives.

No student would put up with such regimen in order to learn social studies or algebra.

Despite the hard work and self-denial, football's popularity is unchallenged by any other participant sport. Each year, the National Federation of State High School Associations conducts a survey of high schools in all fifty states and the District of Columbia to learn which sports have the most participants. Year in, year out, football is No. 1. In 1988–89, for instance, football had 930,034 participants. Basketball, the runner-up, had about half that number.

This book, based on interviews with seven high school players representing both inner city and suburban teams, discloses the special knowledge and technical skills required to play the various positions. It also seeks to explain football's appeal, revealing why the game is so important, even valuable, to so many young men, and why they are willing to work so hard to become good at it.

JARED DOLCE

Linebacker
Punter
Kicker

His coach describes Jared as being "aggressive, a hard tackler, real intelligent, a smart player."

The linebacker has been described as a football genius. What he has to do is figure out what the other team is going to do and then react accordingly.

On running plays into the line, the linebacker has to rush into the thick of things, flinging aside the interference to nail the ball carrier. On pass plays, he has to drift back to cover the receiver. He has to be alert for sweeps and screen passes, for draw plays and rollouts.

9

Name: **Jared Dolce**
Birthplace: **New Rochelle, New York**
Age: **18**
Height: **6′ 1 1/2″**
Weight: **195**
Team: **Fordham Prep Rams; Bronx, New York**
Position: **Linebacker, Punter, Kicker**
Other Sports: **Hockey, Tennis, Swimming**
Favorite NFL Team: **New Orleans Saints**
Favorite NFL Player: **(none)**
Favorite Uniform Number: **22**
Favorite TV Program: **(none)**

Linebackers have only one thing to do: everything.

To play linebacker, you have to be big and fast, tough and smart. It's hard to find a player with all these qualities, but they pretty much describe 18-year-old Jared Dolce, a senior linebacker for the Fordham Prep Rams, who are based in New York City's borough of the Bronx.

Jared has been playing football since fifth grade, when he attended Iona Grammar School (in New Rochelle, New York). He wanted to play linebacker then, but the league in which Iona played had height and weight limitations for most positions. Jared, big for his age, exceeded those for linebacker.

One thing that appealed to him about the position was that linebackers are seldom unsung heroes. Like quarterbacks, they get recognized. Since the linebackers are positioned in between the defensive linemen and the deep backs, they're involved in just about every play and they make most of the tackles. They're the defensive team's heroes. "Like the coaches say," says Jared, "the linebackers are the ones who make All City."

Jared, diverted into playing guard and defensive end in grammar school, didn't get to play linebacker until his freshman year at Fordham Prep. In his junior year, he moved up to varsity status, becoming the only junior on the defensive team.

From the beginning, Jared seemed perfectly suited for linebacker. "It's the best position I ever played," he says. One reason he likes it is because he always knows what's taking place on the field. That's not always true of the other defensive positions. A lineman, bent over in his four-point stance, sees only the player on the other side of the line. The deep backs, the safety and the cornerback, are too far away from the ball to see all that's going on. "But as a linebacker," says Jared, "you can see the whole play as it unfolds."

And a linebacker has more freedom of movement than any of the other defensive players, Jared points out. You go where the action is, rushing in to stop the run, darting back to defend against passes.

Most of all, Jared likes playing linebacker because, as he puts it, "You get to hit; you get to stick people.

"And that's the whole point of football," he adds. "That's what makes it fun."

How important is hitting? Well, Fordham Prep's motto is "To Hit!" At the end of each team meeting following every practice, Jared leads his defensive teammates in a simple chant: "Hit! Hit! Hit!"

"It's a thing that gets everybody going," says Jared. "It gets everybody pumped up."

In his book, *The New York Times Guide to Spectator Sports,* Leonard Koppett writes that football is essentially "a simple game" and "the side that hits harder almost always wins." Jared believes this to be true, so long as one team doesn't have significantly more talent than the other. He says, "If you have two teams that are equal in ability, it's definitely true that the team that hits the hardest is going to win."

Jared knows this from experience. "The team that hits harder wears the other team out by the third quarter," he says. "They don't want to get hit again. They start backing down; they get timid.

"That's what happened in the Riverdale game," Jared says, recalling an opponent that Fordham overwhelmed during his senior year. "We hit 'em, hit 'em, hit 'em! By the end of the third quarter, they were worn out. They didn't want to get hit anymore. It made it easier for us."

Jared has worked hard to excel as a linebacker. He takes practices very seriously. He also sharpened his skills attending a football camp for linebackers during the summer following his sophomore year. The camp was held at Hofstra University in Hempstead, New York, where the NFL's New York Jets practice before and during the season.

"That's where I really brushed up on my skills," says Jared, "I learned *the* tackling technique—to keep your head up, to stay low."

Football camp was also valuable because it helped Jared to improve his ability to "read," to "key," to watch an opponent for some small movement or mannerism that can tipoff the play. "You read the guard," says Jared. "What you do is based on what the guard does. He's going to take you right to the play." If the guard stands up to pass block, it's obvious a pass is coming. You have to get ready to bat it down or intercept.

"If the guard doubles-down, that is, he, along with the center, blocks the nose guard, that tells you there's going to be a blast play into the hole. A lead back is going to hit the hole first, with the tailback getting the ball. You have to step up and plug the hole.

Jared (22) grapples with an opponent during Fordham scrimmage.

"If the guard pulls from his position in the line and races laterally to the right or left, you know he's going to be leading a sweep; you have to shadow him."

While knowing how to read makes it easier for Jared, he can't be guided only by keys. "You also have to watch the quarterbacks and the running backs," he says.

For evidence of Jared's success as a linebacker, all one has to do is glance at his helmet. It's blazoned with decals that document his accomplishments. For every solo tackle or interception a Fordham defensive player makes, he's awarded a skull-and-crossbones decal. There's scarcely room on the right side of Jared's helmet (the side that is reserved for defensive team decals) for any more decals.

A decal in the shape of a football goes to any player who scores a touchdown or boots a field goal. A star is awarded to the player who scores a point after touchdown or to any player on the field when a touchdown is scored.

Jared thinks such decals are a good idea. "They're an incentive," he says. "People work a little bit harder to get more tackles so they can get another decal."

Jared also believes that the decals have an intimidating quality on opposing players. He says: "If you get up against someone who has the whole right side of his helmet plastered with skulls-and-crossbones, you think, 'Oh, my gosh!' I think it works."

Linebacking is only one of several roles that Jared plays. He's also the team's punter and kicker. He is, in fact, with a 38.6-yard punting average, the leading punter in the "A" Division of New York City's Catholic High School Football League. During the 1989 season, one of Jared's punts soared 56 yards (measured from the line of scrimmage).

Jared is largely self-taught as a punter. "I got into a punting groove on my own," he says. One thing Jared did to help himself was watch pro punters on television. "I concentrated on those with the better technique," he says, "those who kicked the ball higher and farther." Reggie Roby of the Miami Dolphins was one of the punters Jared recalls studying. It wasn't until his junior year at high school that Jared first got punting instructions from a kicking coach.

In punting, getting distance is critical, of course, but hang time

Whenever he makes a solo tackle or interception, Jared gets to add a skull-and-crossbones decal to his helmet.

is important, too. Hang time is the amount of time a punt stays in the air. The longer a punt "hangs," the more time the tacklers have to get downfield to cover the receiver. "Our coach is mainly concerned about distance, not hang time," says Jared. "Usually everyone gets downfield right away. Of course, if you can get both distance and hang time, he likes that. Hang time isn't something we concentrate on during practices, but I personally try to work on it."

Punting is no cinch, says Jared. "You can't just stand there flat-footed and kick the ball. The good punters kick *through* the ball, explode through it. Their momentum is so great that both feet come off the ground. I try to punt like that. The difference in exploding through the ball and standing there and kicking it is tremendous."

Besides a strong leg and the ability to kick through the ball, a punter has to be able to kick under pressure. "You have to have poise," says Jared. "If there's a bad snap, you have to be able to catch the ball and still get the kick off. Or if there's a rush on, you still have to be able to make the punt."

As Fordham's place-kicker, Jared kicked off and attempted field goals and extra points. During his senior year, Jared's longest field goal was a 33-yarder.

A soccer-style kicker, Jared never got any special training in place-kicking. "I just learned on my own," he says. "One day in practice, I just started kicking well. It's a finesse thing; I think almost anyone can do it."

During his senior year, Jared played tight end in several games. "They used me in situations where they really needed yardage, situations where they had to throw." And in the season's final game, Jared played fullback. "It went well," he recalls. "I carried the ball thirteen times for 76 yards."

Jared enjoys several other sports, including tennis, swimming,

Dolce tunes up for his role as Fordham's place-kicker.

Dolce takes a break amidst team practice session.

and ice hockey. In hockey, he was seriously injured in a game during the 1987–1988 season. "The whistle had just blown," Jared recalls, "and I was making a turn to my left, my skates parallel, when a kid hit me. My blades stuck in the ice, and my knee went out.

Jared had suffered cartilage and ligament damage to the knee, which required arthroscopic surgery. "It's good now," Jared said of his knee during the football season that followed. "There's no pain at all."

Jared says that playing football has been valuable to him. For one thing, it's taught him self-discipline. "You have to discipline yourself to work hard," he says. "Take homework, for instance. You work like crazy on the practice field for two or two-and-a-half hours after school, and then you're supposed to go home and do a couple of hours of homework. It's like working double time.

"But you can do it—if you discipline yourself. If you go home and have dinner and then just flop down in front of the TV, you'll usually end up falling asleep. The key to doing your homework is to go home, have dinner, and then do it right away.

"Another key is using study period during school hours. In other words, you can't waste any time. You have to schedule your day carefully."

Jared also gives football high marks for helping him to develop leadership qualities. Before the beginning of his senior year at Fordham Prep, Jared was named captain of the defensive team, which gave him the opportunity to gain leadership experience.

For example, during the week before a game, Jared gets the defensive team together in the locker room after practice sessions. He tells the players what the game means, its importance, and what they have to do to win.

During his senior season, when Fordham Prep scored one victory after another, Jared would tell the team how much each opponent wanted to end their winning streak. "Or if we beat a team the year before," says Jared, "I'd tell them the team was out for revenge, out to get us. Or if I happened to hear that a team we were going to play was out running at seven o'clock in the morning to get ready for us, I'd tell them that. Things like that get the team going."

Jared looks forward to playing football in college. His coach believes that Jared is talented enough to play for a major college team.

During the first months of his high school senior year, Jared gave a good deal of thought to the subject. He didn't plan to choose a school simply because it had a topflight football team. He was more concerned about the quality of the college itself. He said, "If I get hurt or decide I don't want to play anymore, I don't want to be stuck in a school I'm not going to like if I'm not playing football."

Does Jared recommend high school football to a boy graduating from junior high or grammar school? He does, but he qualifies his recommendation.

"Football is fun," he says, "and it's something I love to do. But it's also a lot of hard work. You have to realize that.

"You need a great deal of determination. You have to work hard during practice all week. And every night you're expected to go home and do your homework. There's a lot to fit in.

"But when the game comes on Saturday and you're out on the field for the opening kickoff, you forget all about the hard work. In the end, it's all worth it."

BRUCE CAMPBELL

Quarterback
Defensive Back

Although he likes to pass, Bruce usually has to call running plays.

There are two types of quarterbacks, Allie Sherman, former head coach of the New York Giants, once noted. There's the type that, after taking the snap, comes away from the center saying, "I hope I find my receiver." And there is the other, the quarterback who drops back saying, "You'd better stop this one, pal. I'm putting it right there in his gut."

Bruce Campbell is the second type. As quarterback for George Washington High School in New York City, Bruce is confident

Name: **Bruce Campbell**
Birthplace: **New York City**
Age: **17**
Height: **5′ 10″**
Weight: **155**
Team: **George Washington High School Trojans; New York, N.Y.**
Position: **Quarterback, Defensive Back**
Other Sports: **Basketball**
Favorite NFL Team: **New York Giants**
Favorite NFL Player: **Randall Cunningham, Philadelphia Eagles**
Favorite Uniform Number: **4**
Favorite TV Program: **"Cops"**

and bold. When Bruce throws a pass, he *knows* he's going to complete it.

His positive attitude is only part of what Bruce brings to the team. "He's relentless," says Carlos Gomez, the George Washington coach. "He just wants to win. When he does something wrong, I don't have to get on his back about it. He's tougher on himself than I am. He wants to do the best possible. He's driven."

Bruce needs these qualities and more to run the difficult offensive system used by the George Washington team, known as the Trojans. The system is based on the wishbone formation, a variation of the T formation in which the position of the four backfield men gives the Y-shaped appearance of a wishbone. The fullback lines up a couple of yards directly behind the quarterback. The other two backs, the right halfback and left halfback, are positioned a few yards behind the fullback and set to his right and left.

The Trojan team has been using the wishbone since the early

Bruce is valuable, says his coach, for the positive attitude he brings to the team.

1980s. "The wishbone is an offense you use when you don't have big offensive linemen," explains Coach Gomez. "Most of the kids that go to this school are Hispanic. So we don't get linemen of tremendous size such as other schools get. On offense, we depend on speed and deception—and we get that from the wishbone."

You have to be skilled and smart to direct the wishbone. On each play, Bruce has to read the moves of the defensive linemen and decide whether to keep the ball himself or pitch back to one of his running backs. The option to keep the ball or not is presented three times on each play. In fact, some coaches refer to the wishbone as the "triple option."

It works like this: Once Bruce has taken the snap from center and checks what the defensive tackle is doing, he either hands the ball to his fullback or keeps it himself. If he decides to hold onto the ball, he follows the fullback to the right or left, reading the defense as he goes. If a defensive player moves up to tackle him, Bruce tosses the ball back to one of his halfbacks. Bruce's third choice is to either keep running until he's brought down or drop back and fire a pass.

Bruce praises the wishbone for keeping the defense honest. "The defense doesn't know who's going to get the ball," he says, "and they don't know where the ball is going."

While Bruce says that the wishbone has worked well for the team, he complains that the system restricts him by not giving him enough opportunities to throw the ball. It's a running offense; Bruce thinks of himself as a passing quarterback.

What Bruce dreams about is running an offense such as the run-and-shoot, where the quarterback passes the ball well over 50 percent of the time. He points out that University of Houston quarterback Andre Ware, winner of the Heisman Trophy in 1989 as the outstanding player in college football, was a run-and-shoot quarterback.

Bruce realizes, however, that being a ball-carrying quarterback has certain advantages. For one thing, it could be a plus factor as far as college is concerned. "Colleges run a lot of wishbone," he says, "so they're looking for quarterbacks who know how to move around and at the same time can throw the ball with accuracy. They're not looking for the classic, drop-back passer. So I guess the running experience I'm getting will help me a lot. But I still like to throw the ball."

The Trojans are a hard-working team. They practice five times a week. They also, like virtually all teams today, rely on sports psychology to improve their performance. The players and coaches feel the difference between winning and losing can be a mental difference.

Two approaches have worked for the team. Bruce describes them: "Sometimes on the night before a game, the team gets together, and we go to the football field. And we sit there on the field in the dark. We talk about the game and what we have to do to win. We try to develop the closeness that we're going to need the next day.

"And the next day, not long before the game, we turn out the lights in the locker room, and we play the tape we have of Phil Collins singing 'In the Air Tonight.'

Campbell (foreground) leads the Trojans in up-downs.

Bruce and Danny Reyes (right), one of his favorite receivers.

"We used that song during my junior year and we won the City championship. Everything is quiet, except for the tape. And all we're thinking about is winning. It gets us real psyched up—we get crazy, you could say. It's not a blind rage, because we have to think about what we have to do on the field. But we're very angry. We want to win the championship, but that team is in our way."

Bruce first became interested in football when he was attending elementary school at P.S. 173 in Upper Manhattan. "I used to like to run back kicks and punts, dodge guys out," he says. "They didn't know where I was going."

He became a quarterback almost out of necessity. During his first year at George Washington High School, Bruce was a defensive back and running back for the freshman team. When the varsity quarterback graduated, the team's coach sought out Bruce for the position. "I guess he had seen me throwing the ball around," Bruce says. In his first varsity season, Bruce led the Trojans to the championship of the Public High Schools' "B" Division.

The team had high hopes of repeating as titlists the following year but finished out of the running with a 5-2 record. The loss of players through graduation had weakened the team, Bruce feels. "We lost some breakaway speed out of the backfield," he says. "And our offensive line wasn't the same. All but one lineman graduated."

Playing high school football in New York City is no easy matter, Bruce says. He feels that New York players are disadvantaged. In other parts of the country, Bruce has observed, football programs are much different. Not long ago, Bruce visited Marion High School in Marion, South Carolina. "You know," he says, "they have four or five weight rooms there. The team gets extra jerseys, jerseys just for practice, new helmets, practice helmets, and practice pants. They give the kids jackets, T-shirts, sweat suits, and warm-ups. The kids get a lot of things we don't have up here.

27

"The junior varsity has four or five coaches. The varsity has ten coaches, including scouting coaches. At George Washington there are only two varsity coaches. And we have only one weight room, and that's for the whole school to use; we don't have our own weight room.

"Another thing other schools have is night games. I *dream* about playing at night. Lights; the stands are packed. We play most of our games in the morning, at eleven o'clock. So not that many people come to the games. They should play at 2 o'clock or 3 o'clock. We'd have more fans.

"And up here we don't get all that rah-rah you get down South. I see high school sports on TV, and I see all the parents out there, big crowds, banners, and a band at the game. Up here, there's not a lot of school spirit. Sometimes it makes you feel bad when you're playing out there.

"You get national exposure at these schools, too. We don't get that. They say we don't play real football because we live in the city. But I think that's cockamamie." As evidence, Bruce cites several players who have graduated from George Washington in recent years and gone on to play football at top-ranked colleges. He names Miguel Aquino, who plays second string for the University of Oklahoma and Miguel Guzman, second string at Ohio State. Other former Trojans are playing football at the University of Nebraska and Indiana State University. "When I hear about these players," says Bruce, "it makes me think I can do it."

When it comes to the academic qualifications colleges seek, Bruce should not have any problem. He is one of the better students at George Washington, a member of the school's honors program. Social Studies and English are his favorite subjects. He thinks he'd like to be an accountant one day. He might major in that subject in college.

Whether or not his career provides a path to college, Bruce

Campbell watches during a scrimmage. "Football can teach you a lot of things," he says.

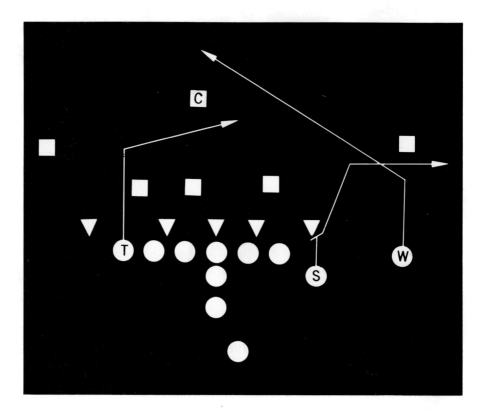

This is Bruce Campbell's favorite play. A pass play designed for long yardage, it's called Sam Right, Slot Right, 623.

Bruce takes the snap and rolls to his right. The wide receiver (W) breaks straight downfield for ten yards, then veers toward the goalposts. The slotback (S) brush-blocks the defensive end, spurts downfield for five yards, then cuts for the sideline. The tight end (T) heads seven to ten yards downfield, then races straight across the field in back of the linebackers.

The play is intended to outwit the cornerback (C). If the cornerback moves to cover the wide receiver, Bruce throws to the slotback. If the cornerback covers the slotback, the wide receiver should be open. If one of the other defensive backs should cover the slotback and the cornerback covers the wide receiver, Bruce has his tight end to throw to.

As Bruce rolls out, he scans his receivers from right to left. During his senior year, Bruce called this play four times and it produced a long gain each time. Twice it resulted in touchdowns.

still feels football has been worthwhile. He says: "You learn things from football that carry on for the rest of your life, things you have to do. You learn to do things on time. You learn to discipline yourself." Bruce's coach says that he hasn't missed a practice in two years and he always arrives on time.

"I've learned there are no individuals on the team. Everyone is a team player.

"You become closer to the people around you. You make friends with the other players. Because football is a team sport, there's a closeness that comes from playing that you don't get from baseball or basketball or other sports.

"When you win, the whole team wins," he says. "It's a feeling everyone gets. When you get your butt kicked, everyone gets their butt kicked."

Bruce draws a parallel between football and life. "In life, you're going to have a family. And the family members have to stick together. They have to have certain values. Football is like that.

"Everyone thinks that football is for jocks, for dummies. It's not at all. Football can teach you a lot of things."

JIM LITTLE
Offensive Tackle

While Jim Little is dedicated to football, his studies are No. 1.

Of all the players on a football team, none are more anonymous than the members of the offensive line, particularly the two tackles and two guards. To the people watching, they're usually nameless, unknowns.

Newspaper accounts of a game usually concentrate on the winning quarterback, the running backs, pass receivers, and perhaps the kicker or punter. A defensive player who makes a key interception or tackle might also get to see his name in print.

Name: **Jim Little**
Birthplace: **Manchester, Connecticut**
Age: **17**
Height: **6′**
Weight: **250**
Team: **Enrico Fermi Falcons; Enfield, Connecticut**
Position: **Offensive Tackle**
Other Sports: **Powerlifting**
Favorite NFL Team: **New York Giants**
Favorite NFL Player: **Anthony Munoz, Cincinnati Bengals**
Favorite Uniform Number: **29**
Favorite TV Program: **"Cheers"**

But offensive linemen remain as unrecognized as the grounds-
keeper who lays down the chalk lines before the game.

Part of the problem results from the fact that the offensive
linemen are about the only players for whom there are no
statistics. Passers' achievements are documented by comple-
tions, runners have their yardage stats, and defensive linemen
compile sacks, tackles, and assists. Kickers and punters also
have their accomplishments recorded numerically. But there's
no statistical attention paid to offensive linemen, no matter what
they might happen to achieve.

Jim Little, a junior offensive tackle for the Enrico Fermi Falcons of Enfield, Connecticut, is very aware that outside of the
practice field and playing field, no one pays very much attention
to him or his colleagues in the offensive line. It even carries over
into his social world. "When we go to parties or other kinds of
get-togethers," he says, "the pass receivers and running backs
always seem to have the girl friends. We [the offensive linemen]
just sit there and talk to one another."

Little gets ready for a Falcon practice session.

The lack of recognition doesn't bother Jim. It goes with the territory, he feels. The coaches know what he's doing. So do his teammates.

His job, he realizes, is to protect the quarterback and block for the runners. "If they get their names in the paper, then I feel I've done my job," Jim says. "That's all the recognition I need."

This is the kind of statement one expects from someone who plays in the offensive line, and Jim is very typical. Offensive linemen tend to be quiet and serious about what they do. They seldom complain.

To those who coach and play football, or even to some of those who merely watch it, there is a marked difference in character between defensive and offensive players. Green Bay Packer coach Vince Lombardi, as quoted by Paul Zimmerman in his book, *A Thinking Man's Guide to Pro Football,* once put it this way: "An offensive lineman usually has a technical approach to the game. He can be trained and developed. A defensive player can get by on instinctive reactions and emotion."

Jim agrees with this. But he puts his feelings in stronger terms. "Defensive players are usually psychos," he says. "They're nut cases.

"The offensive lineman has different assignments on each play. He has to do different things—keep the defensive player away from the quarterback on some plays, block for the ball carrier on others. He can't get emotional. If he did, he'd forget his assignment. He'd mess up. The offensive lineman has to think more.

"Someone with a defensive player personality is more aggressive," Jim says. "He's more inclined to make things happen. A person who is a natural offensive player is more willing to accept things as they are; he's more laid back."

Offensive guards and tackles toil in virtual secrecy, despite the fact they have a tough job to do. One thing that makes it tough is trying to keep the defensive players away from the quarterback as he's setting up to pass. Pass blocking, it's called.

It's awkward to pass block. It bears little resemblance to the classic method of blocking in which a player uses his body to cut down an opponent to clear a path for the ball carrier. In pass blocking, you have to stay on your feet, using the upper body and arms to keep the player opposite you from reaching the passer.

"You have to bend your knees and get down in a half-squat position," Jim says. "You have to keep your back straight and pull your neck back.

"Imagine you're sitting on a straight-back chair and someone takes the chair away," Jim explains. "That's the position you're in when you're pass blocking. It's kind of hard to get used to it."

The hands are weapons. The offensive linemen lashes out with his hands at the defensive player opposite him, jabbing him, pushing him, trying to control him. "You can only use the palm of your hand when you're pass blocking," Jim says. "The movement has to be very quick. You give the guy slight pops."

The feet also play an important role. At the same time Jim is holding his head and upper body erect and striking out with his hands, he is "chopping" his feet—moving them up and down fast, like he's running in place.

"If you're stationery and flat-footed, an opponent can push you backward or shove you to one side," Jim says. "But when you're chopping your feet, it's easier to keep your balance. And when you lash out at an opponent, it's easy to go in any direction he goes."

Jim's duties as a pass blocker are made doubly difficult by the run-and-shoot offense the Falcons use. On most teams, the pass blockers retreat to form a "pocket," a semicircle of protection

Little practices backpedaling during Falcon agility drill.

for the passer. But with the run-and-shoot, the quarterback is on the move, rolling out to his right or left on every play, with the option to run or throw. But he doesn't run very often, not the way the Falcons play the game. The Enfield team passes the ball 60 to 70 percent of the time.

The linemen have to move with the quarterback, move laterally. If the quarterback moves to his right, the play-side linemen have to take a half step to the right before they block.

The linemen on the other side of the line, the back-side linemen, execute a hinge block, pivoting so as to keep themselves in between the quarterback and the defensive man on the other side of the line. "We're told to imagine there's a camera on our rear ends, and we're to keep that camera pointing at the quarterback," says Jim. "In other words, our back is always toward the quarterback, while at the same time we're facing the defensive player."

On running plays that go toward his side of the line, Jim's job is not quite so difficult. His assignment is usually to seal off the defensive end, that is, prevent him from getting to the ball carrier or the ball carrier's blockers.

Jim first became interested in playing football when he was 12 years old. He tried out for the Enfield Stars, a team in a local recreational league. Jim wanted to play defensive tackle but he was too big. The weight requirement for the position was 135 pounds; Jim weighed 150.

Jim dieted and did extra running but he couldn't get down to the required level. "I felt bad," he recalls. "I worked hard and practiced with the team, but I never got a chance to play."

Jim played soccer that fall and then tried football again as a high school freshman. He quickly won a position as an offensive tackle.

Freshman football was child's play for him. "I had a ball," he says. "I just went out there and hit people." But as a sophomore, he found things different. There was a great deal to be learned. By comparison, freshman football was just a start, a period of orientation. As a sophomore player, he had to work much harder; he had to develop an assortment of blocking techniques.

One thing in Jim's favor was his size. He's always been big. Today, at 6 feet and 250 pounds, he's about the biggest player on his team.

Offensive tackles have to be big and tall to be able to cope with the towering defensive ends whom they face. It's standard procedure for the end to use his hands and arms to try to pull or jerk the tackle one way or another. "He tries to throw you around," Jim says. If the tackle should happen to be smaller than the end, he'd be at a great disadvantage.

It's also helpful to the quarterback to have tall tackles. "It gets him used to throwing over obstacles," Jim points out. "When a tall end comes toward him, his arms upraised, it's no big deal. The quarterback doesn't feel as if he's throwing over a building, or something."

Jim's favorite pro player is Anthony Munoz, an All Pro tackle for the Cincinnati Bengals, a member of an offensive line that's been called an "elephant stampede." Munoz is 6-foot-6 and weighs 278. Jim tunes in anytime a Bengal game is telecast in his area, concentrating on Munoz and the other offensive linemen. "I notice how they always stay low," he says, "how well they move their feet and how they're able to move people out of their way."

If Jim ever got a chance to talk to Munoz, he'd ask him how he got to be so quick, and how he's able to keep his feet moving all the time. And Jim would like to know the kind of weight training program Munoz used to get as strong as he is.

Weight training plays a vital role in Jim's training program.

Weight training is an important aspect of Jim's life. He began with a program that stressed simply body building. But he was never happy with it. It emphasized lighter lifting, that is, lifting relatively small amounts of weight a great number of times. This served to improve the quality and tone of his muscles but did little to increase his strength. What Jim wanted to do was heavy lifting, which he knew would make him stronger.

Once he began powerlifting, Jim made remarkable progress. Take the push press, a drill in which you stand erect, your feet about shoulder-width apart, holding the bar just below your chin, so it's touching your upper chest. You bend the knees, then straighten up and thrust the bar straight over the head until the arms are fully extended. You pause for a second, then lower the bar to the starting position. When Jim started, he could barely press 100 pounds. By the end of the summer, he could press 250 pounds.

He also found that he could shove people around—if he wanted to. It was easy for him to pick up objects he previously had found heavy, such as an air-conditioning unit or either of his parents.

During the football season, Jim, along with other members of the Falcon team, work out with weights twice a week. The rest of the year, it's four times a week for Jim, a two-hour session each time.

Jim would like to become as strong as he possibly can, developing his potential to its fullest. For instance, in the bench press, an exercise in which you lie down on your back (on a weight bench) and extend the bar straight above the chest, Jim would like to be able to press at least 300 pounds. As for the push press, described earlier, Jim wants to be able to press 600 pounds before he graduates from high school. "That's about average," he says.

Becoming very strong isn't Jim's only goal. He's also concerned about developing greater quickness.

Jim says that when he gets beat by a rival lineman, it's almost always because the player is quicker than he is, not stronger. "Sometimes a guy will breeze right by me," Jim says. "It's discouraging."

Jim runs the 40-yard dash in 5.6 seconds. He'd like to be able to do it in 5.0.

"But," he says, "my first three steps are very quick—and that's what's important."

Jim advises young players to learn how to run fast and develop quickness. "Work on your speed," he says. "That should be first. If you don't have speed and quickness, it's going to be tough."

To improve his own quickness, Jim jumps rope. He also runs sprints. In fact, in team practice sessions he sometimes is made to do so much sprinting that he feels as if he's going to collapse. "Sometimes I think I can't make it," Jim says. "But you can't quit. And you can't complain, either. You can't start saying, 'All this running stuff sucks; the coach is a jerk.' Once you start saying things like that, you're fighting yourself. You're also fighting the team. People that do that really don't want to be here."

While Jim's life seems to be centered on football and the hard work necessary to play it well, he is also very much concerned about doing well in his studies. Although he hasn't missed a practice in two years, Jim says that if he ever had to study for an important test and practice interfered, he'd cut practice. And if he ever had to choose between playing football and getting a good education, he'd choose the latter.

"If you have good grades, you can do anything you want," Jim adds. "It's like having speed and quickness. It's what comes first.

"If you don't have good grades, it doesn't do any good to be a superathlete. What can you do with your life?"

Jim gets a tip from Falcon assistant coach Mike Marino.

FELIX VALDEZ

Halfback
Safety

Valdez gets suited-up for a team practice session.

To be a good halfback, it takes, first of all, size and speed. And the player has to be durable, that is, able to avoid injury. And, of course, the position requires knowledge; you have to know the blocking assignments and the routes to run on pass plays.

But most of all, running with the ball takes natural ability. There's very little you can learn from an instruction book. You

Name: **Felix Valdez**
Birthplace: **San Francisco de Macoris, Dominican Republic**
Age: **18**
Height: **5′ 8″**
Weight: **185**
Team: **George Washington High School Trojans; New York, N.Y.**
Position: **Halfback, Safety**
Other Sports: **Basketball, Baseball**
Favorite NFL Team: **New York Jets**
Favorite NFL Player: **Freeman McNeil, New York Jets**
Favorite Uniform Number: **24**
Favorite TV Program: **"Doogie Howser, M.D."**

can't teach a player to start fast, to run with balance, to avoid tacklers; you can't teach moves.

Felix Valdez, a rough and rugged halfback for the George Washington Trojans, agrees. "They can teach you to stay low and avoid contact," he says, "but that's about it. Running is what you think and what you do at that moment. It's instinct."

Felix also says that you can improve, however, that you can get better with experience. "Say I hit a hole on an off-tackle play," he explains, "and I want to go outside. Well, first, I'll make a move to the inside. That gets the linebacker to react, to hesitate. Then I can swing to the outside. That kind of thing comes with experience."

When it comes to football, the amiable Felix has an unusual background. He was born in the Dominican Republic, where baseball is the national sport and football is almost unheard of. Felix's family moved to New York when he was three years old, and he grew up there. He lives with his mother and a cousin in an apartment in the Washington Heights section of New York. Felix and his cousin, who is five years older than he is, are very close. "I call him my brother," says Felix.

When Felix was very young, his cousin, who had attended George Washington, would take him to see football games there. "They were alumni games—old-timers," Felix recalls. That was Felix's introduction to the game. Today, his cousin still attends Trojan games, but nowadays it's to watch Felix play.

"The first time I saw football, I fell in love with it," Felix recalls. What he likes is the intensity, the hitting. Whether he's carrying the ball or angling for a tackle on defense, he does it with enthusiasm. "The hitting—it's fun," he says. "If you hit the way you hit in football when you're out on the street, you're breaking the law; you'll get arrested."

"Always do your best, try your hardest," Felix tells young players. "But have fun, enjoy yourself."

Hitting is the game's essential ingredient, Felix believes. During his junior and senior years at George Washington, the coach would sometimes ask him and other veteran players to speak to the incoming freshman, the junior varsity team. On such occasions, Felix would say this: "The name of the game is hitting. You can't be afraid to hit; you gotta get used to it. If you can't hit, you can't play."

Felix learned about football from pickup games he played on city streets and in local parks with friends and relatives. "I always played with older kids. I was the youngest of the group," he says. "So I think I learned the game faster than most kids.

"I always wanted to be a running back," Felix says. When you're carrying the ball, you get to hit first, instead of having someone hit you."

Felix's first experience in high school football wasn't a happy one. The coach yelled at the players a great deal. "He was always yelling," Felix recalls. "I didn't get along with him very well." After his freshman year, Felix transferred to George Washington High School.

"The coach at Washington yells, too," says Felix, "but you get the idea he's only doing it because he wants you to do better."

Felix tells young players they have to learn to accept criticism from the coaching staff. "Don't get down on yourself," he says. "When the coach yells at you, don't take it personally. Yelling is part of the game. Try to do better next time."

After arriving at George Washington, Felix played fullback. But during his senior year, the coach moved him to his present position, left halfback. "He needed someone bigger to play fullback," Felix says. Felix's speed and size—he's powerfully built but of no more than average height—were better suited for playing halfback.

Felix and his teammates enjoy playing for Carlos Gomez, the

Behind stout blocking, Valdez (24) runs for daylight during team scrimmage.

George Washington coach. The 32-year old Gomez grew up in the same Manhattan neighborhood as his players and he once played football for the Trojans. "He's one of us," says Felix.

Felix also likes the wishbone, the offensive system used by the George Washington team, because it gives him plenty of opportunities to carry the ball. At the other high school where he played, the coach had installed a "pro slot," a passing formation. "I was getting only six or so carries in a game," Felix says. With the wishbone, Felix gets twice as many.

Felix has a goal every time he's handed the ball. He may try

48

to get a first down; he may try for a touchdown. It depends. During an intrasquad scrimmage, Felix carried the ball on a sweep. It was third down, and the team needed five yards for a first down. As Felix raced to his left and sized up the blocking, he felt he had a chance for a long gain, perhaps even a touchdown, by turning downfield and following the sideline. But then he saw a crack of daylight to his right—a chance for a first down. He cut back and darted through the hole for a ten-yard gain. "That's what we needed the most, a first down," he says. "That's what we needed at the time."

49

In the wishbone system, Felix is often called upon to block on plays he calls "triples"—triple option plays. The quarterback, after taking the snap, hurries to his right or left, following the fullback. When the play goes to the right, the right halfback gets the pitch and Felix leads the play. "My job is to take out the end," he says. "It's the key block. If I don't make it, the halfback can get cut down in the backfield."

Felix also has a route to run on pass plays. The Trojans throw ten or twelve times during a game. Usually the quarterback targets on Felix when he finds his other receivers are covered. "I'm a safety valve," Felix says.

Felix also plays on defense; he's a strong safety, meaning that he lines up opposite the tight end. "They call the position 'rover,'" says Felix, "but I call it strong safety; it sounds better."

When playing defense, Felix keys on the running backs. "Wherever they go, I go.

Felix says he's always involved in a lot of tackles. In a key game during his junior season, Felix made no less than seventeen tackles. "I was coming up into the line a lot," he says with a grin, "and I happened to have a good day."

When it comes to defense, Felix is a "scrappy kid," according to Coach Gomez. "He has a tremendous desire to play," says the coach, "and he really makes things happen."

In a game during his senior year, the opposition completed a pass when Felix was out of position. On the very next play, the team tried the pass again. But this time, Felix was in the right place. He made an interception and returned the ball for a touchdown.

"He has a lot of heart," says the coach. "He's one of those kids who gives me all he has."

Playing both ways, on defense as well as offense, requires

great stamina. The Trojans do sprint drills to help build endurance and Felix does a great deal of running on his own, especially during the off-season. He and his cousin run together on an average of three times a week, jogging through a local park or visiting a dirt track where they run sprints.

"I play basketball during the summer, too," says Felix, "and baseball and softball. I'm never quiet. I'm always playing something."

Felix also exercises the year 'round with free weights, barbells and dumbbells. During the football season, he works out with weights twice a week at school, but when he's not playing football, he trains with weights six times a week at a local gym.

Each day, he focuses on a different part of his body. One day may be devoted to leg exercises. The next, he might concentrate on his upper body. He'll do bench presses, inverted bench presses, dumbbell presses, and flyaways, or flys, exercises in which dumbbells are raised and lowered while lying on one's back.

Felix says he does "pretty well" in school. Math is his favorite subject. He also likes computer courses. "Studying is hard," he says, "especially during the season. When you come home from practice, you're tired. You have to force yourself to work."

Felix looks forward to going to college. He's not sure, however, whether he's going to be offered a scholarship, although two colleges expressed interest in him during his senior year. "It's hard, very hard, coming from the City," Felix says. He feels that he and many of his teammates don't have the background and experience in football that native-born American boys have, and this places them at a disadvantage.

In addition, he says, the kids in New York get almost no support from the community. They lack playing facilities and equipment. "These kids grow up playing touch football on concrete," Felix says. "They don't get to play 'real' football until they go to high school. They don't know the game."

As evidence, Felix cites Francisco Soriano, who plays right halfback for the George Washington team. Francisco, who was born in the Dominican Republic and brought up in Puerto Rico, didn't see his first football game until he was 14 and a freshman at George Washington. When he tried out for the junior varsity, Soriano not only won a starting position but he was named team

Felix (left) has a word with Francisco Soriano, also a halfback for the George Washington team.

captain. A fast and elusive runner, Soriano later became a stand-out performer for the varsity team. Felix calls him a "great player," despite the fact he's been playing only a relatively short time. "If he had started playing as a young kid, he'd be even better," says Felix.

"And that goes for me, too," he adds.

If he does get a chance to continue his education, Felix would like to attend a college outside New York City. He and his mother recently visited a family friend in Boston and Felix had a chance to tour the Boston University campus. "Boston would be nice, real nice," Felix says with a grin. "It's peaceful there, it's quiet, much different than New York. "It's the kind of place where you'd like to go to school.

STEVE KRATIS

Defensive Tackle
Offensive Tackle

Steve Kratis, who plays offensive tackle as well as defensive tackle, prefers playing defense.

A great offense doesn't always make for football success. It takes more than a gifted quarterback, sure-handed receivers, and backs who can run with speed and power. A team has to be tough on defense, too. Whether its high school or professional football, the best defensive teams are always in the race for the championship.

The defensive team begins with the front four—the two tackles and two ends. The linebackers are stationed behind the front

Name: **Steve Kratis**
Birthplace: **Hartford, Connecticut**
Age: **17**
Height: **6′**
Weight: **210**
Team: **Enrico Fermi Falcons; Enfield, Connecticut**
Position: **Defensive Tackle, Offensive Tackle**
Other Sports: **Baseball**
Favorite NFL Team: **Dallas Cowboys**
Favorite NFL Player: **Howie Long, Los Angeles Raiders**
Favorite Uniform Number: **77**
Favorite TV Program: **"NFL Game Day"**

four and the safeties and cornerbacks are deeper still. But it all begins with the front four. If they're able to keep pressure on the passer and jam the holes on running plays, it makes it easier for everyone else. The linebackers can drift back and help out on pass defense. The deep defensive backs can use more deception in their coverage and be more aggressive in going for the ball.

Calling the front four "defensive" players isn't really accurate. That implies they're standing around waiting to beat off an aggressor. That's not the case at all. When the ball is snapped, each tackle and end attacks, driving into the lineman opposite him, using his hands, arms, and shoulders, kicking and clawing, if necessary, the idea being to get the quarterback or stop the run.

For big and rugged Steve Kratis, defensive tackle for the Enrico Fermi Falcons of Enfield, Connecticut, playing defense is what makes football fun. "I love it," he says. "It's aggressive; you get to attack. You get to hit someone instead of getting hit." As Steve describes it, the difference between playing defense and

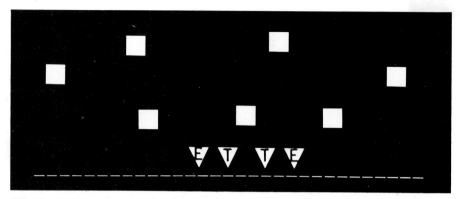

The front four—two ends (E) and two tackles (T)—anchor the defensive team.

playing offense is somewhat the same as the difference between an evildoer and his victim.

When the ball is snapped, Steve reads the quarterback to determine whether the play is going to be a run or a pass. "If it's a run, you try to get into the hole and stop the running back," he says. "If it's a pass, you try to get by the offensive lineman and go for a sack."

In getting past the lineman opposite him on running plays, Steve usually tries to jerk the player in whatever direction he wants to go. "Sometimes he'll lead you to the play," Steve says.

When the play is a pass, Steve sometimes uses what he calls the "swim technique" to get through, grasping the blocker by one shoulder, then the other, and shoving him to the ground. All the while, the offensive man is trying to fight Steve off, lashing out at him with his hands and arms. "He can almost punch you in the stomach," Steve says.

Steve has to watch constantly for sucker plays. The trap is one. The offensive player will allow Steve to come rushing in. Then

Hands in front of body, knees bent, Steve drills on stance for pass blocking.

suddenly he'll be blocked from the side by a pulling guard or tackle.

You have to read when you're going to be trapped. "If the offensive man doesn't block you, you know it's coming," Steve says. "Then you have to set up, stay low, and take on the trap. You have to prepare yourself to get hit and hit back. Don't let the offensive player attack you; attack him."

Steve recalls a game during his junior season when the opposition used a trap unexpectedly. "I got hammered," Steve says. "I was standing up, facing the quarterback, when the offensive man came from the side and cleaned my clock."

Steve has to be alert for screen passes, too. When the opposition tries a screen pass, Steve and the other defensive linemen are allowed to penetrate. When they're within an arm's length or so of their prey, the quarterback flips the ball out to his right or left to a receiver who's shielded by a wall of blockers.

"When a screen pass is coming, the coach usually yells out to warn us," Steve says. "I guess he can tell by their formation and the game situation."

"Defense is more exciting," Merlin Olsen, formerly a defensive tackle for the Los Angeles Rams and later a broadcaster on NBC-TV's football telecasts, once said. "On offense you're part of a machine. Defense is more individual."

Steve agrees with this, but only in part. "It depends on the situation," he says. "When you're making a goal-line stand, you feel like you're involved with a team. But other times, like when you're trying to make a tackle or block a pass, you go for individual achievement.

"But on offense, you're always working as a team. Everyone has to make their block in order for the play to work."

Steve can speak with authority on the merits of playing offense as opposed to defense because he does both. He's also an

Kratis (center) hits the blocking sled during Falcon practice session.

offensive tackle for the Falcons. And he does more. He's a special team specialist. He's a member of the punting team—"I block first, then go down and attack"—the punt return team, and the kickoff return team. He's on the field for extra point attempts and field goal tries. In fact, the only time Steve's not on the field is when the Falcons are kicking off.

All that playing time means Steve has to have plenty of stamina. "I'm in good shape," he says. "The coach sees to it that we all run a lot in practice.

"We really don't begin to get tired until the fourth quarter. But if we let down in the fourth quarter and get outscored, we get punished. During the next week at practice, we have to do extra sprinting, running an extra 100 yards for every point we were outscored. And we have to do it not one day but everyday." That means if the Falcons should be outscored by 6 points in the fourth period, each player has to do six 100-yard sprints each day of practice the next week.

"We try to stay strong," Steve says with a grin.

When it comes to building endurance and strength, weight lifting is very important to Steve and virtually all his teammates.

Steve chats with teammate Donny Clark. Falcon decals are awarded for fumble recoveries, sacks, passes batted down, and other standout plays.

During the off-season, Steve visits a local gym five times a week to lift weights. Each session lasts about ninety minutes. Specific goals are usually involved. Says Steve: "If I've been bench pressing 200 pounds, my goal at the end of the month might be to bench 225 pounds." Or his goal might involve repetitions, the number of times he can lift a specific amount of weight without stopping.

During the season, Steve and other members of the squad lift weights two afternoons a week following football practice. These sessions last about forty-five minutes.

During Steve's junior year, the Falcons won their first seven games of the season, then lost to a strong Rockville, Connecticut, team. Steve attributes the loss to the fact that the Rockville players were more dedicated as weight lifters, that, as a group, the team lifted weights during the off-season. "We have a couple of guys that went to the gym and lifted," he says, "but their whole team went. That's what made the difference.

"They were physically stronger than we were. They just pounded us. We were beat up by the fourth quarter. Emotionally, we just died.

"The guys that are stronger are going to win," says Steve.

For a boy coming out of junior high school and planning to play football in high school, Steve has this advice: "Lift weights," he says.

He also suggests working on quickness and agility. He recommends several drills. "Hopping, just hopping, will do it," he says. "I know it sounds funny, but hopping up and down on one foot and then the other helps your footwork. Skipping rope is also good."

The Falcon team has several drills to improve quickness. "We chop our feet," says Steve. "We do it every day." Chopping one's feet is similar to running in place, only it's done very fast. The

Steve (right) awaits ball's snap during Falcon scrimmage.

feet pound up and down but they don't come very far off the ground. "It's like you're trying to stomp on ants," Steve says.

To pick up playing tips, Steve suggests watching football on television. He recommends college football, not professional. "The pros tend to take it easy," he says. "But the college players don't. They're always trying to impress someone. The pros are already there so they don't have much to worry about.

"I notice the enthusiasm of college players," says Steve. "That helps me a lot." From the standpoint of enthusiasm, Steve gives Notre Dame high marks. When the Fighting Irish come out on the field, Steve notes, "They're like a time bomb ready to explode.

"When you watch a game, don't watch the ball; watch the linemen," Steve suggests. "You might be able to learn a new blocking technique or the way to get away from a blocker." Steve recalls once seeing Howie Long, a defensive lineman for the Los Angeles Raiders, using what he calls a "rip technique." It's a move similar to delivering an uppercut in boxing in which the right hand is used to raise the left arm of the offensive lineman. "It's a real good move," says Steve.

Reggie White of the Philadelphia Eagles is another pro player Steve enjoys watching, and Michael Dean Perry of the Cleveland Browns is a third. "They're real quick," Steve says.

Not only has football helped Steve to develop physically, it's also helped him in developing his character. "You're disciplined all the time," he says. "You can't screw around in school because you'll get punished for it."

Steve describes himself as a "B and C student." He adds, "We have to keep our marks up in order to play football." The coach receives a weekly progress report on each player in each subject. If a player looks to be failing a subject, special tutoring is arranged for him.

Keeping low, Kratis gets set to launch a block during Falcon practice.

"We have to refer to the coach all the time as 'sir.' We have to say, 'Yes, sir,' and 'No, sir.' That teaches you discipline.

"If you screw around in practice, they make you run extra. If you don't get your assignments right, the whole team may have to run, and you don't want that to happen. You don't make many friends when you cause the whole team to run.

"If you're late for a meeting or late getting out on the field for a practice, they'll make you run. Any little thing, they'll make you run."

Running extra can mean running what's called a gym drill. A player or the entire team runs from one sideline to the nearest hashmark, reaches down to touch the hashmark, then runs back to the sideline; then runs to midfield, touches the ground, and returns to the sideline; then runs to the far hashmark, touches it and returns to the sideline; and then, finally, runs to the far sideline, touches it, and returns to the starting point.

A player being punished for some infraction of the rules may have to run as many as three gym drills, that is, run the whole sequence three times.

"One time we had to do it five times," Steve recalls. "That was at the beginning of the season. That was not a good practice. I went home and collapsed."

The running and the extra running, the practice sessions, the weightlifting after practice, and the games take their toll. "At the beginning, it's great," says Steve. "Until about the eighth week of the season, it's great. Then you start getting tired. By the end of the season, you're tired all the time.

"It's kind of a relief when the season is over. For the first month or so, you just feel like going home and sleeping after school. You're drained. You try to come back to life."

The discipline and hard work have not diminished Steve's love for the game, however. He looks forward to playing the game as a senior and, later, in college. Whether or not he's offered a scholarship, he realizes, depends on his performance as a senior. He hopes he plays well enough to attract the attention of college scouts.

But he intends to play in college whether or not he gets a scholarship offer. "If I don't get a scholarship, I'll just try out," he says. "Most definitely, I'll play again. I want to."

CHARLES ANDRUSS
Quarterback

Andruss is a good passer but prefers to call running plays.

Everyone knows it takes a good arm to be a successful quarterback, the ability to throw short and long. And it requires poise and intelligence. You have to be able to read defenses and then call formations and plays accordingly. It takes some running ability, especially in high school and college, meaning the quarterback has to be tough and durable.

It also takes the ability to lead. The coach may be in charge

Name: **Charles Andruss**
Birthplace: **Bronxville, New York**
Age: **16**
Height: **6′**
Weight: **170**
Team: **Fordham Prep Rams; Bronx, New York**
Position: **Quarterback**
Other Sports: **Baseball, Basketball**
Favorite NFL Team: **Pittsburgh Steelers**
Favorite NFL Player: **Terry Bradshaw, Pittsburgh Steelers**
Favorite Uniform Number: **12**
Favorite TV Program: **College football**

of things, but the quarterback is the field general. He gives the commands out there; the other players obey.

When it comes to leadership, Charles Andruss, quarterback for Fordham Preparatory School in New York's borough of the Bronx, excels. His coach says he helps the team by what he says as well as by what he does. "He's a born leader," says his coach.

Charles, the youngest of three children, all boys, doesn't lead by being bold and aggressive or by barking out commands like a Marine drill sergeant. He does it with his quiet confidence, with a word of encouragement or a pat on the back.

Charles, who was born and brought up in New York's Westchester County, north of New York City, took over as Fordham's quarterback at the beginning of his junior year. He had quarterbacked the junior varsity the season before and the freshman team the year before that.

Charles was nervous before his first few games as varsity quarterback, but it didn't show in the game results. The team kept winning one game after another.

But about midway in the season, with the team still un-defeated, Charles had what he calls a "terrible game." He had trouble passing and threw two interceptions. "I just didn't throw the ball well," Charles recalls. "There was no zip on it."

In the game that followed, the coach called fewer pass plays than he had called earlier in the season. Charles began to be-lieve that the coaches were questioning his ability. His confi-dence dwindled. "I got down on myself," he recalls.

Part of Charles's problem was the pressure he felt as a junior surrounded by seniors who wanted to win the division cham-pionship. He sometimes worried that some of the older players would resent it if he tried to show too much authority. Charles said: "Sometimes I'm afraid I'm going to tell them something and someone is going to say, 'Who is this guy? He's only a junior.'"

The coach helped Charles get back on the right track. He stopped criticizing Charles during practice sessions and didn't yell at him as often as he once had. "He wasn't on my case that much," Charles recalls. "He made it easier for me."

And the coach put in more pass plays. Charles's confidence began to return.

Being confident is essential, Charles says. You have to believe in yourself. "If you're not confident, it affects the other players. When you're in the huddle, you can tell it by the expressions on their faces."

Charles is always encouraging his teammates in an effort to boost their confidence. "The coaches are pretty tough on the linemen and backs," Charles says. "So I try to be nice to them. When a lineman makes a good block, I pat him on the back. 'Nice goin', I say."

Before a game in which the Fordham team was favored late in his junior season, the coach told Charles that he was going to play him only during the first half, that he planned to use the

Of his coach, Ron Lombardi, Charles says, "He yells, and then it's all over. You know he doesn't mean it."

team's backup quarterback, a sophomore, during the second half to give him some game experience. It was a nondivision game, and thus the outcome would not count in the division standings.

In the first half, Charles guided the team to a 14-0 lead. Then the sophomore quarterback took over. He immediately threw an interception, which the opposition turned into a touchdown, cutting Fordham's lead to 14-6. The coaches screamed at Charles's replacement as he came off the field following the interception. Charles went up to him. "Don't worry about it," Charles said. "The coaches are always yelling. Try to relax. Try to forget about it."

When the sophomore quarterback got back into the game, he threw another interception, and again it led to a touchdown by the opposition. That made the score 14-12. "I could see he was really down," Charles recalls. "I tried to make him feel better. I told him the next time it would be different, that he wouldn't have any problems."

Andruss gets ready for a Fordham scrimmage with this leg-stretching drill exercise.

Later in the game, the backup quarterback threw a touch-down pass, and Fordham went on to an easy win. "I felt really good about the touchdown pass," Charles says. "It showed me he didn't get down on himself."

Charles realizes the importance of getting emotionally pre-pared for a game, but he follows a routine of his own. He watches the other players as they go through their pregame rituals, exchanging back slaps and helmet slaps and chanting, "Hit! Hit! Hit!" Charles understands the importance of this, but he likes to keep more to himself. "I think about what I have to do as the quarterback, being a leader," he says. "I think about what I have to do to help the team win—about the plays we're going to use and what I have to do on each one. I think about the patterns the kids are going to run on pass plays.

"I think about being really calm and showing I'm ready for the game."

In other sports he plays, Charles also tries to set an example. Take basketball, for instance. Charles plays forward for the Ford-ham Prep team but he's not a starter. "I'm the first or second man off the bench," he says. "But when I'm on the bench, I cheer for the team. And when I get into the game, I may not score points but I do other things well, like playing tough defense and rebounding, things like that."

In baseball, it's the same. "When I'm out in left field, I'm yelling for the pitcher, telling him to throw strikes, trying to get the team psyched up."

Charles didn't start out in football as a quarterback. When he was in third grade, he played as an offensive lineman for a team in a Scarsdale, New York, recreational league. He also was a running back. But when he arrived at Fordham Prep several years later and saw how big all the linemen were, Charles decided to change the direction of his football career. That's when he made up his mind to become a quarterback.

Charles, like virtually all the members of the Fordham team, is involved in weight training. He began lifting not long after he joined the team and realized how much weight work the other players had been doing.

The summer before his junior year, Charles worked out with weights three times a week, using facilities available at the school. He concentrated on strengthening his upper body, particularly his throwing arm. A Fordham coach supervised the program.

"You have to be big to play high school football nowadays," Charles says. "You have these big linemen who work with weights all the time. I'm not the 'superweight' type. I don't have weights at home. But as a quarterback, I have to keep up with these big defensive guys. Otherwise, I'm going to get hurt."

The Rams operate out of the I formation, a variation of the T formation in which one of the halfbacks and the fullback line up in tandem a few yards directly behind the quarterback. The other halfback is flanked out to the right or left. The I formation is a good formation to use to get a fast back to the outside in a hurry. It's well suited to Fordham's basic strategy, in which some 70 percent of its plays are running plays.

The head coach sends in the plays that Charles is to call in the huddle, using ends as messengers. It's up to Charles to modify the play, according to how the defense lines up. For example, suppose the messenger end brings in a "wham" play from the sidelines, a plunge into the line with a back leading the ball carrier. When the team breaks from the huddle and Charles goes up to the line of scrimmage, he scans the defense. He may notice there are more defensive backs on the right side of the field than the left. When he gets up behind the center to take the snap and

Charles (11) hands off to a fast-moving back during Fordham practice drill.

calls out the signals, he instructs the ball carrier to hit the left side of the line, the side where the defense is the weakest.

Charles plays no role on defense. That's OK with him. He likes to be able to focus on what he has to do as quarterback.

As a sophomore, Charles did occasionally play safety, and he also did some place-kicking for the team. But as a junior, the coaches, fearing he might get injured, asked him to give up these duties. "The coaches don't like to have the quarterback playing defense," Charles says. "They're afraid someone on the other team might give me a cheap shot, and I might get hurt.

"Plus," he adds, "I don't tackle that well." He recalls a game during his sophomore year in which he missed a tackle on a kick return, a slipup that resulted in a touchdown for the opposition. "I think they've kind of given up on me as a defensive player," he says.

Charles says he does "pretty well" in school. He takes seven subjects and is a "B" student.

"The schedule during the week is very tight," he says. "I get up and go to school. My mother, who works at the school as the attendance officer, drives me. After classes, I practice. I get a ride home with one of the other players. I have dinner, do my home-work, and go to bed.

"Sometimes it's really tough. But I try to keep my grades up."

Charles feels he's profited from football in several ways. For one thing, he's gained many friends through the game. He re-calls his first year at Fordham Prep. He and his teammates-to-be were asked to arrive at the school a week before the semester began to start football practice. "That gave me a chance to get to know all the kids on the team," Charles says. "It was a head start. By the time school began, I had all these friends." In the years since, he and other members of the team have gotten to be "a close group," Charles says.

Football has also enabled Charles to become more persistent, more tenacious; he's acquired a mental toughness from football. Charles remembers a game against Riverdale in which the Rams were 11-point underdogs. In an effort to catch their highly touted opponents off guard, Fordham planned a no-huddle offense. They would run one play after another in quick succession, with Charles calling each play from the line of scrimmage.

The strategy backfired. "Gosh, we were really terrible," Charles says. "On our first series of downs, we couldn't move the ball at all. Then, when we punted, Riverdale blocked the punt, recovered the ball, and scored." Fordham trailed, 6-0, and the game had scarcely begun.

On the sidelines, Fordham regrouped. The team abandoned their no-huddle offense and went back to its conventional running and passing game.

Fordham scored a touchdown to tie the game. After the two teams exchanged touchdowns, Fordham scored two more touchdowns to win, 24-12.

Playing football is exciting to Charles. He says: "The pass plays, the big gains, the touchdowns—that stuff is great!"

He realizes that playing quarterback is an advantage. "Everything is centered around you," he says. "You make the decision and everything goes from there. Everything goes back to the quarterback."

During Charles's junior year, the championship of the division went undecided until the final game of the season in which Fordham faced its traditional rival, Xavier High School of Manhattan. Xavier led, 14-0, as the game came down to the final minutes. Then Charles led a stirring Fordham comeback. After driving the Prep team 45 yards in three plays, he fired a 39-yard touchdown pass to Tom Greco. After Fordham failed in the extra point attempt, Xavier led, 14-6.

Tom Greco (left) is Charles's favorite receiver.

After the touchdown, Fordham regained possession of the ball by means of an onside kick. Charles led the Rams downfield again. Two passes from Charles to Tom Greco—one for 17 yards, the other for 12 yards—brought the ball to the Xavier 6-yard line. From there, Charles knifed his way into the end zone.

Again Fordham failed to convert. Xavier now led, 14-12. Only 2 minutes, 42 seconds, remained.

After Xavier was stopped on downs, Fordham took over the

Charles Andruss's favorite play is a pass play called Wing Right 26 Blast. It can be used almost anytime the team is in between the 30-yard lines.

There are three receivers—two ends (E) and a wingback (W). The wingback lines up one yard behind the line of scrimmage and a yard to the right of the right end. He races seven yards downfield, then cuts across the middle.

"I fake a handoff, then drop back and throw," Charles says. "I look for the wingback first. If he's covered, I check the other receivers." During his junior season, Charles passed for several touchdowns using this play.

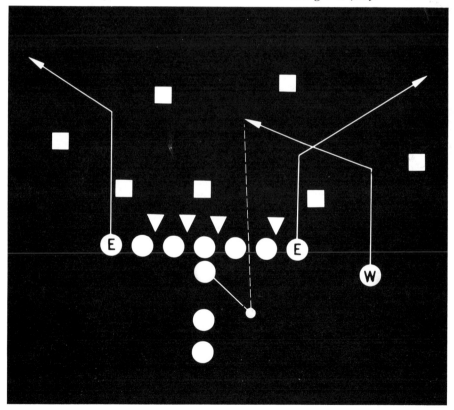

ball. Passing and running, Charles steered his team deep into Xavier territory a third time. The home crowd was on its feet and screaming. "They really got into it," Charles recalls. The ball was on the Xavier 17-yard line; 48 seconds were left to play.

Charles tried one pass and then another. Both went incomplete. Twenty seconds remained. "Throw a touchdown or throw it out of bounds," his coach told him.

Charles took the snap and sprinted to his left, his arm cocked to throw. He spotted Tom Greco in the end zone. Just as he was about to let the ball go, a Xavier defenseman barrelled toward him. Charles gave ground, throwing off-balance as a result. The ball was short of the target and a Xavier back raced up to intercept, sealing Fordham's defeat.

It took several days for Charles to shake off the loss. "It was tough," he says.

But he felt good about the season as a whole, a season in which the Rams ended with a 6-3-1 record. "The season was great," Charles said. "We showed people we could play. It would have been awesome if we had won that last game.

"Everyone is up for next year. We're going to be better. It's going to be our year. We're looking forward to winning the championship.

"We're confident. I just hope we're not *over*confident."

MIKE KELLY

Split End
Safety

To Mike Kelly, football is fun. But it's not his whole life, he says.

Pass receivers come in all shapes and sizes—and speeds, from medium fast to jet-propelled. Mike Kelly, split end for the Enrico Fermi Falcons of Enfield, Connecticut, isn't the fastest pass receiver in the world nor, at precisely 6-feet, the tallest. But he has good speed, sure hands, and knows how to make a catch in heavy traffic.

Quiet and modest, Mike also has a very positive attitude about his job. When he goes out for a pass, he reads the defensive back that's covering him and adjusts his pattern accordingly. "If the defensive guy is playing in close, I run straight by him," Mike says. "If he's playing deep, I turn left or right. If he's playing inside, I go outside, and if he's outside, I go inside." It's as simple as that, according to Mike.

Mike's favorite pattern is what is called a post corner. On this, he breaks five or six yards straight downfield, veers toward the middle of the field for a couple of steps (toward the goalposts, or post), and then suddenly cuts in the other direction, slanting toward the corner of the field. "It's impossible to cover," Mike says. "When you take the two steps to the inside, the cornerback turns his hips and starts running in the wrong direction. When I suddenly change direction, he can't recover in time."

When it comes to reaching up and making the catch, Mike, who always wears receiver's gloves when he plays, says that

When making a catch, concentration is the key element, according to Mike.

concentration is the key. "You can't think about getting hit," he says.

Anticipation is important, too. Mike says: "Always look for the ball. You never know when it's coming."

Mike also plays safety for the Falcons. In fact, he prefers playing defense. "It's a lot better," he says. The reason: "You don't get hit; you *give* hits."

Mike had no formal football experience before he went to high school. He was introduced to the sport as a freshman. "Some of my friends were on the team," Mike recalls, "and told me it was fun, and that I should come out." He played running back and safety as a freshman.

Mike's problems as a freshman player were few. "I had played some football, like pickup games in the street, so I knew a little bit about the game," he says. "It wasn't that hard to learn. Besides, the freshman players weren't that good."

Freshman coach Mike Marino, later to become the varsity team's line coach, was there to help. "Coach Marino gave me the basics," says Mike. "He told me where I should be positioned, where I should be going, and what I should be doing.

"We'd have meetings before practices, and we'd go over the plays we were going to use. The coach would diagram them on the chalkboard. The plays were all pretty much the same so they were easy to remember."

During Mike's sophomore year, the team had an abundance of running backs, but there happened to be a shortage of receivers, so the coach suggested Mike become a split end. There was another factor. Mike was stretching out, becoming taller and slimmer. Running backs have to be big and strong to power their way through the line or break tackles. Mike was beginning to look more like a pass receiver.

As a sophomore player, Mike found football a bit more difficult. Now he was being matched against varsity players, junior and seniors. They were more experienced. "And they were bigger, a lot bigger," Mike recalls. "And quicker, too."

The team had difficulties, too, struggling to a 3-6-1 record. "We were terrible. We started out good, but we fell apart," Mike says. "The team wasn't together. Many of the players didn't like one

Kelly unlimbers—with the help of a teammate.

As a defensive back, Mike has to be skilled in backpedaling.

another. The sophomores and juniors were good friends, but we really didn't like some of the seniors."

The following season, when Mike was a junior, the team did a complete turnaround, winning their first seven games. Then, after a couple of defeats, the team rebounded to trounce its traditional rival, Enfield High School.

For someone beginning football as he did, as a high school freshman, Mike has two pieces of advice. "Don't quit," he says. "Even though it can get hard sometimes, don't quit.

"And never be afraid to ask questions. When I was starting out and we were in different defenses, I'd ask where I should be positioned or who I should be covering. You can do like I did—if you don't want to ask the coach, you can ask other players."

When it comes to pass defense, the Falcons use each of the two basic types—man-to-man and zone. When the team employs man-to-man, each deep defensive back is responsible for covering a specific receiver. When using a zone, each defensive player has a specific area of the field to cover.

"When we play a passing team, we use man-to-man," says Mike. "When we play teams that run the ball a lot, we use zones."

Mike prefers man-to-man. It causes fewer problems. "In man-to-man, you pick out the guy you're going to cover, and then just follow him. In the zone, three guys can come into the zone you're covering."

While Mike almost always plays safety when the Falcons take over on defense, he is sometimes assigned to play cornerback, the other deep defensive position. He says there's not much difference between the two positions, although cornerback is more likely to present a critical moment now and then. "You can get beat much easier at corner," Mike says.

It's because as a cornerback, Mike has a clear-cut set of responsibilities, a particular receiver to pick up or a specific area of the field to cover. If the receiver that comes Mike's way happens to have bullet speed, it's possible for him to blow right by Mike. Then it's his fault; there's no one else to blame.

Playing safety is somewhat different. "When someone else on the defensive team messes up, I pick up the open man," Mike says. Not only is his assignment easier, but as safety he plays deeper than when at cornerback. There's more time to adjust.

Mike's favorite NFL player is Hanford Dixon, a defensive back for the Cleveland Browns. He sometimes watches Cleveland games on television and focuses on Dixon in an effort to pick up playing tips. Dixon, like all deep backs, backpedals as a receiver breaks into his zone, then turns to run with the man. Watching such a play unfold can be helpful. "You can learn to make your turn," says Mike, "when to stop backpedaling and move to cover."

Mike looks forward to playing football as a senior. "The games are fun," he says. "But I also like just being on the team, being with everybody."

The varsity players have status, too. "Everybody around the school knows the team, knows the players," Mike says.

But Mike is somewhat dubious about his future in football beyond high school. If he should happen to be offered a scholarship, he says he'd play football in college. But he doesn't think he can meet the standards of a Division I or Division II school, which are the foremost football colleges, according to the classification system of the National Collegiate Athletic Association (NCAA).

Mike feels he lacks in both size and speed. He points to the fact that he runs the 40-yard dash in 5 seconds. "You have to run like a 4.3," he says. More height would be helpful. But Mike, now a six-footer, thinks he's only going to grow another inch or so.

If Mike does play football in college, he feels it will be for a

Twice a week, football practice sessions are followed by weight work.

Division III college. But that presents a problem. "There aren't a lot of good schools in Division III," he says. "And I want to go to a good school. I'd like to go to a good state school, such as North Carolina State."

If Mike does attend such a school, he doesn't think he'd try out for the football team. He'd put his career on the shelf.

"I like football," Mike says. "But it's not my whole life."

GLOSSARY

AUDIBLE—A substitute offensive play or defensive formation called at the line of scrimmage out of a need to adjust to the deployment of the opposing team.

BACK—*See* Defensive Back, Offensive Back

BLITZ—An all-out rush by one or more of the linebackers and defensive backs in an effort to sack the quarterback or force him to hurry his throw.

CENTER—The player in the middle of the offensive line who snaps the ball back between his legs to begin each play.

CORNER PATTERN—A pass route run toward one of the corners of the field.

CORNERBACK—One of usually two defensive backs who lines up behind and outside the linebackers, and whose chief responsibility is to cover a split end on pass plays.

COVER—To guard a receiver in an effort to prevent him from catching a pass.

CURL—A pass pattern in which the receiver runs downfield and then loops back toward the line of scrimmage to catch the ball.

DEFENSIVE BACK—One of usually three or four players—cornerbacks and safeties—positioned behind the linebackers, and whose chief responsibility is to defend against passes and breakaway runs.

DOUBLE-DOWN—A defensive formation in which the center and one of the guards are both assigned to block the nose tackle.

FULLBACK—An offensive back positioned behind the quarterback who is usually assigned to carry the ball or block.

HALFBACK—A member of the offensive backfield who is assigned to carry the ball, block, or receive passes.

HASHMARK—*See* Inbounds Line

I FORMATION—An offensive formation in which the backs are aligned generally in the shape of the letter I, with the quarterback directly behind the center and two running backs in tandem a few yards directly behind the quarterback.

INBOUNDS LINE—One of the lines parallel to the sidelines that are marked on the playing field at the yardlines, and that are used in spotting the ball when the ballcarrier goes out of bounds over a sideline or when the ball is punted or fumbled over a sideline.

KEY—A tip-off or indication of what the opposing team intends to do on a particular play; also, to watch an opposing player for a clue to the intentions of the opposing team on a particular play.

LINE OF SCRIMMAGE—The imaginary line that runs from sideline to sideline through the ball and separates the offensive and defensive teams.

LINEBACKER—One of several defensive players positioned a yard or two behind the line of scrimmage who is responsible for filling holes in the line to stop the ballcarrier and defending against short passes.

MIDDLE GUARD—*See* Nose Tackle

NOSE TACKLE—A defensive lineman positioned in the middle of the line between the defensive tackles and opposite the center; also called a middle guard.

OFFENSIVE BACK—One of usually four players—the quarterback, fullback, and two halfbacks—positioned behind the line.

OFFENSIVE TACKLE—One of two offensive linemen positioned outside the offensive guards who is responsible for opening holes for runs or pass blocking.

ONSIDE KICK—A kickoff in which the kicking team attempts to maintain possession of the ball by recovering the kick after it travels the required minimum distance of 10 yards.

OPTION—An offensive play in which the ballcarrier has a choice of running with the ball or passing it.

PASS BLOCK—To protect the passer by blocking on a pass play.

PATTERN—Any pass route run by a receiver.

POST PATTERN—A pass route in which the receiver angles toward the goalposts.

PULL—To pull back from one's position in the line to lead the blocking on a running play or trap block a defensive player.

READ—To determine the intentions of the opposition by observing player movement or position.

RUN-AND-SHOOT—An offensive system in which the quarterback rolls out to his right or left with the option to pass or run.

SACK—To tackle the quarterback as he is attempting to pass.

SAFETY—One of usually two defensive players positioned directly behind all of the other players and responsible for protecting against passes or long runs.

SLOT—In the offensive line, the gap between an end and a tackle.

SLOTBACK—A running back who lines up behind the slot.

SNAP—Action on the part of the center in which he hands or passes the ball back between his legs to begin a play.

SPLIT END—An offensive player positioned at the line of scrimmage several yards outside the other linemen as a pass receiver.

SWEEP—An offensive play in which the ballcarrier runs around the end behind blockers.

T FORMATION—The offensive formation in which the backs are aligned roughly in the shape of a T, with the quarterback positioned directly behind the center, the fullback four or five yards behind the quarterback, and the halfbacks on either side of and slightly ahead of the fullback.

TAILBACK—The deepest positioned offensive back.

TRAP—A blocking maneuver in which a defensive player is allowed to penetrate the offensive line, and is then blocked from the side by a pulling guard or tackle.

WINGBACK—A running back who lines up just to the outside of the formation and serves as a pass receiver.

WISHBONE—A variation of the T formation in which the halfbacks are positioned to either side of and slightly behind the fullback (in roughly a wishbone alignment).

INDEX